P9-DOA-927

Adam & Thomas

Text © 2013, Aharon Appelfeld

Originally published in Hebrew as *Yalda Shelo Minhaolam Hazé* (A Girl from Another World).

English-language translation © 2015 by Jeffrey Green

First English-language edition October 2015.

Seven Stories Press
140 Watts Street
New York, NY 10013
www.sevenstories.com

Library of Congress Cataloging-in-Publication Data

Apelfeld, Aharon, author.
  [Yalda Shelo Minhaolam Hazé. English]
  Adam and Thomas / by Aharon Appelfeld ; translated from
Hebrew by Jeffrey Green ; illustrated by Philippe Dumas. -- A
Triangle Square Books for Young Readers edition.
      pages cm
  Summary: Adam and Thomas, two nine-year-old Jewish boys
who survive World War II, take refuge in the forest where they
learn to forage and survive, soon meeting and helping other fugi-
tives fleeing for their lives.
  ISBN 978-1-60980-634-7 (hardback)
1. World War, 1939-1945--Juvenile fiction. [1. World War,
1939-1945--Fiction. 2. Jews--Fiction. 3. Survival--Fiction.
4. Refugees--Fiction. 5. Holocaust, Jewish (1939-1945)--Fiction.]
I. Green, Yaacov Jeffrey, translator. II. Dumas, Philippe, illustrator.
III. Title.
  PZ7.1.A64Ad 2015
  [Fic]--dc23
                          2015010371

Printed in China

9 8 7 6 5 4 3 2 1

Adam & Thomas

Aharon Appelfeld

translated from the Hebrew by Jeffrey M. Green

illustrations by Philippe Dumas

Seven Stories Press
New York • Oakland

Chapter 1

They walked quickly, hand in hand, and at sunrise they reached the edge of the forest. "Adam, dear," said his mother, "we're there. Don't be afraid. You know our forest very well, and everything that's in it. I'll try very hard to come this evening. But if I'm late, go to Diana's, and I'll come later and pick you up."

Adam stood next to his mother, still drowsy, and he didn't know what to ask. His mother repeated: "Don't be afraid. You know our forest very well, and everything that's in it. Sit down under a tree, like that one with the round top, read the book by Jules Verne, or play jacks. The time will pass quickly."

His mother hugged him and said, "I have to run. I'm going to hide your grandparents." She slipped out of his arms and set out. Adam stood where he was. He wanted to call out, "See you

5

later, Mom," but he didn't manage. His mother was already out of sight.

The forest was waking up, and the first rays of light scattered on the ground. Adam walked forward slowly. He knew the trees and the paths, but still this was a slightly different forest: an early morning forest. He was used to coming to the forest with his parents, usually in the afternoon, and sometimes toward evening, but never early in the morning.

"Strange," he said to himself. "I'm walking in the forest by myself."

Meanwhile he reached the tree with the round top, placed his knapsack at his feet, looked around, and said, "Nothing has changed here. It's the same forest, except my parents aren't with me."

Adam was nine and about to finish fourth grade. He wasn't an outstanding student, but on his last report card three A's stood out, which pleased his parents, and they bought him a new soccer ball.

The war and the ghetto had put an end to walks in the forest. For a moment he was happy that his mother had taken him out of the walled-in ghetto. She had brought him here and was sure he would manage by himself.

A stream ran near the tree. It was still covered

in thin darkness, but spots of light flashed on the flowing water.

Adam felt hungry and took a sandwich out of his knapsack. The sandwich was wrapped in brown paper. Adam remembered how his mother had stood next to the kitchen window and sliced the round loaf of bread to make him sandwiches.

They had left the house at dusk. They went from cellar to cellar, scurrying through dark tunnels, crawling in narrow places, and at last, after an effort, they had come out of the darkness into a field. They crossed the Johann Bridge and in a few minutes they were at the edge of the forest.

"You know our forest very well, and everything that's in it." He heard his mother speaking to him again. Now he sat down and looked at the light spreading at his feet.

Suddenly he rose, knelt, scooped some water from the stream with his hand, and brought it to his mouth. The chilly water tasted good. He kept drinking until his thirst was slaked.

"Interesting," he said. "Mom's not here, but I can see her clearly, and I feel her hand in mine."

He had come to this enormous forest with his father and mother in the spring and summer. They had trees they liked to sit under, streams whose water they liked to drink. Miro used to run and skip and add his joy to the pleasure of the walk.

"Miro!" Adam called out. Suddenly he could feel the dog's round body in his hands. Everybody loved Miro. He wasn't as big as a German shepherd, but he filled the house, and even when he was napping in the entrance, he was alert.

Now Adam saw the house, the carpentry shop, his father and mother, and his grandparents, and Miro jumping from place to place, or standing still in surprise. The more he saw those familiar sights, the more his fear died down. His eyes closed, and he fell asleep.

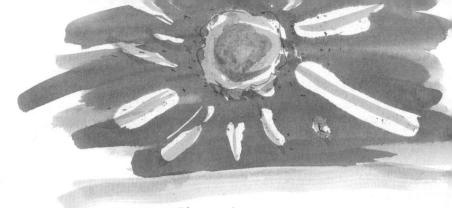

Chapter 2

When he woke up, the sun was already high in the sky. In his sleep he had been at home, in the kitchen, and for a moment he wondered how he had come to the forest, but he immediately remembered that his mother had brought him and told him: "We're there. Don't be afraid. You know our forest very well, and everything that's in it." Her sentences echoed in his mind for a moment, and they pleased him. Adam was very familiar with the forest in the afternoon. After a day of work, his parents went out to refresh themselves among the trees. His father carried sandwiches, cake, fruit, and vegetables in his backpack. His mother put two thermos bottles in her long handbag, with coffee in one and hot cocoa in the other.

Adam used to look forward impatiently to these excursions. In the forest his parents were relaxed. They conversed and listened to each other. In the end all three of them would play ball.

After an hour of play, Adam's shirt would be wet, and his mother would say, "You're absolutely soaked. Too bad I didn't bring a change of clothes."

For a moment Adam felt sad because he was alone. He went back to the stream, sipped some water, took an apple out of his pack and bit into it. The bite brought his father and mother back before his eyes, and he felt they weren't far away.

While he was wondering what to do and where he would go, he heard noises. He pricked up his ears: the noises sounded like shuffling through dry leaves.

He couldn't see a thing from where he was sitting. He rose to his feet, and to his surprise, not far off, a boy was walking heavily, with a pack on his back.

"Hello, boy. Who are you, and what are you doing here?" Adam called out loudly.

"My name is Thomas," the answer came quickly.

"Come over here."

"Here I am."

Once he was close, Adam saw he was a class-

mate. "Who brought you here?" Adam asked in a friendly way.

"Mom brought me here this morning and told me to wait for her. Since then I've been wandering around the forest and getting tired."

"My mom also told me to wait for her. Let's wait together," said Adam, smiling.

"Strange," said Thomas.

"What's strange?" asked Adam.

"Suddenly we're alone."

Thomas removed the pack from his back, sighed like a grown-up, and sat down.

"Have you eaten already?" asked Adam.

"Not yet. I'll do it now. I'm hungry."

"I've already eaten, and I drank from the brook."
Thomas pulled a sandwich out of his pack and
bit into it.

At school Thomas sat in the first row, because
he was nearsighted. Now you couldn't tell he was
nearsighted, maybe because of the green cap that
changed his looks.

"Have you been here long?" Thomas asked.

"I got here early in the morning with my
mother. The forest was still dark."

"Weren't you afraid?"

"No, I know this forest and everything that's in
it." Adam repeated his mother's words.

"It's lucky you spotted me. I was getting discouraged."

"Actually I didn't recognize you."

"I didn't recognize you either. But that's not
saying much. To my regret, I'm nearsighted," said
Thomas.

Adam noticed the words "to my regret."
Thomas was a polite boy and often said "excuse
me" and "thank you."

"I'm glad we're together. While I was alone, I
didn't feel good. I was sure I'd get lost. By the way,
when did your mother promise to come back and
get you?" Thomas asked.

"In the evening."

"My mom also promised me she would come in the evening. The two of us will go back home together," said Thomas, and he was glad he had said those words. "My mom sent me with too much. My pack is as heavy as a flour sack."

"My mother also equipped me as if I were going on a long hike. What isn't there in my pack? Bandages, iodine, aspirin, two boxes of matches, and lots more," said Adam.

"I don't even know what's in my backpack."

Chapter 3

Adam remembered that his mother had told him, "If I don't come by the evening, go to Diana's house." Strangely, perhaps because of the emotional meeting with Thomas, he had forgotten that instruction.

Diana helped his mother at home, but she was a bitter woman, silent, and it always seemed that she was about to burst out and shout.

"What are you thinking about, Adam?" Thomas asked.

Adam told him.

"My mom also told me to go to Diana."

"Diana's going to open a home for abandoned children," said Adam, and they both laughed.

"I don't like Diana," said Thomas.

"Me neither, but there's no choice. In the ghetto they snatch up children."

"Let's wait for our mothers until the evening. Then we'll see."

Since first grade, Thomas had attracted Adam's attention. First, for his nearsightedness, later for his other qualities. Because of his fastidious character and his constant excellence in school, Thomas wasn't popular. His classmates teased him, and he tried to defend himself with what he knew: the arithmetic exercises, the compositions that he wrote, the books that he read. But those efforts only increased resentment against him. The teachers tried in vain to protect him. In the end his classmates ignored him and acted as if he didn't exist. Thomas suffered. You could see his suffering in everything he did, even the way he walked. Did Adam also take part in the general ill-treatment? Not actively, but he hadn't stood up for Thomas.

Once Adam met him in the street and asked how he was. Thomas was surprised that one of his classmates spoke to him, and in his embarrassment he said, "What do you want from me?" Then Adam said to him, "If you don't do so well, they won't mistreat you." That sentence upset Thomas, and he said, "What should I do?"

"It's very simple. Don't stand out. Your good

grades make the other students uncomfortable."

"Okay," said Thomas, and he slipped away.

Right after that meeting, Adam was sorry for what he had said to Thomas. It seemed to him that he'd hurt his feelings, but he didn't go back to him to apologize.

Since then they hadn't spoken.

It was strange that Thomas was the one God had sent to him, the thought flashed through Adam's mind. The religion teacher, Brother Peter, always used to say that there were no coincidences. Everything happens for a reason. If you met someone, that was a sign you were supposed to meet him, a sign that you would get something from him that you lacked. Don't ignore those meetings. There's a message of discovery in every meeting with people.

Not only did Adam hear the religion teacher's words, but he also saw him standing there, dressed in his monk's habit and different from other people. Meanwhile, Thomas fell asleep.

Chapter 4

The sun was setting, and red lights glowed on the treetops. Adam clearly remembered this hour, when he would sit under this tree with his parents. It was always an hour of soft light.

His father, an expert carpenter, would tell them a story from his army service or a secret of his craft, or he would describe something funny about one of his customers.

The carpentry shop was next to their house, and Adam used to spend long hours there. He liked the beams and boards, the power saw, and the tools his father used to carve and smooth the wood. Adam also liked the sawdust and its fragrance.

After his father finished assembling a table, he would stand and look at it from a distance. Then he would say, "I put quite a bit of myself into this. I doubt whether the buyer will appreciate that."

His mother helped his father with sanding and polishing and applying lacquer. Before the Jewish holidays, they would work until late at night.

Now Adam took in what he might not have taken in before, the closeness between his parents. They liked listening to each other and didn't argue.

Thomas woke up with a start, looked around, and cried out, "Where am I?"

"You're in the forest with me." Adam knelt beside him.

"Sorry, in my sleep I was at home."

"Now you're here. Don't worry."

Thomas glanced at his watch and said, "It's eight o'clock. Where are our mothers?"

"Let's wait and see. The days are long during the summer. Darkness won't fall until ten or eleven." Adam tried to comfort Thomas. "I suggest that we eat supper. Our mothers will come, and they'll find us eating. That will please them."

"Excellent idea," said Thomas.

There was a thermos of cocoa in Thomas's backpack. On the lid, which was also a cup, was written, in his mother's handwriting, "Close tightly."

They each ate one of their sandwiches, and Thomas offered Adam a cup of cocoa.

"Excellent cocoa," said Adam after sipping some. "Thank you."

"You're welcome."

"Strange," said Adam, "just last spring I sat under this very tree with my parents. Dad was taken to the labor brigade. Mom is trying to hide my grandparents, and I'm here. Everyone in a different place."

"My dad was also taken to the labor brigade. Since Dad was taken, Mom hasn't been able to sleep. She's awake all night," Thomas told him.

Darkness spread around the tree trunks, but in the depths of the forest some patches of light still glimmered. Thomas looked worried. He didn't hide his worry and asked Adam, "Are you sure our mothers will come and get us?"

"My mom keeps her promises, and I assume yours does, too. But you have to take the danger into account. The ghetto is shut tight. The watchtowers shine bright searchlights on the area. Most of the ways out are through cellars, and they've posted guards over them, too."

"Since the war began, everything has changed," Thomas said, sounding like a grown-up.

"Our parents haven't changed. They were and will be our parents forever," Adam said, surprised that such a sentence had left his mouth.

Chapter 5

After that, darkness covered the forest.

"Let's make a nest in the tree," Adam suggested, and a spark lit in his eyes.

"You're joking, Adam," said Thomas, laughing.

"Our tree is solid. It's made of lots of thick trunks that twist about and rise up. They make a dense, strong top. We can cover the top with branches and spread a blanket over them."

"And if our mothers come, will we see them?" Thomas asked.

"From up above you see a lot better."

Adam climbed the tree, and Thomas handed him branches and leaves. Adam cushioned the top and called down from above: "Soon we'll have a great nest."

Thomas handed him the backpacks, and Adam helped him climb the tree.

"Wonderful, Adam," Thomas showed his enthusiasm.

"Sometimes it's a good thing to learn from the birds." Adam spoke like a craftsman whose skill had succeeded.

"You're right. From up here you can see better. I have a blanket in my backpack, and I bet you have one, too. We'll spread one blanket on the branches, and we'll cover ourselves with the other," Thomas tried to contribute his part to the initiative.

"A great idea," said Adam.

They lay down to see whether the nest would bear their burden without caving in.

"Have you ever slept in a treetop before?" Thomas asked.

"No, but I've put up a tent with my parents, and we slept in it."

"When our mothers come to get us, they'll be amazed at your invention, Adam."

"It's already dark. They'll certainly come in the morning. I'm tired," said Adam.

～⌒

As they were closing their eyes, they saw a man running through the forest. "It's a good thing we're up here," said Thomas. "There's no way of knowing what the runner would do to you."

"Somebody who's running is busy running and won't pay attention to you," Adam surprised him with his insight.

Then silence prevailed. Here and there an owl screeched, but except for that, not a sound was heard. Adam fell asleep. Thomas couldn't sleep. He was awake and saw his father and mother before his eyes, and the people who came and went in their house.

Thomas's father, a tall man, nearsighted like his son, was a high school teacher. His mother taught in elementary school. During the ghetto time, before he was taken to the labor brigade, he continued to teach his students at home, after they were suspended from school. "Study preserves us," he would reply to everyone who expressed doubt about his efforts. "Particularly at this time, we have to protect our souls," his father would repeat.

Thomas's mother made sure he kept at his studies, and Thomas did work hard on arithmetic exercises, he read books, wrote compositions, learned poems by heart, and in the evening his mother would examine him and say, "Excellent. You've made good progress."

All during the long days in the ghetto, Thomas plunged deep in his studies. He heard and knew what was going on around him, but the arithmetic exercises and the reading filled his soul. He didn't understand that he had to prepare himself for a new life until his mother announced she was taking him to the forest the next day. What would it be like? He couldn't imagine.

Adam hadn't studied during the time in the

ghetto. He helped his mother, who was working in the communal kitchen. He peeled potatoes and beets, sliced cabbage, and washed pots. At noon a long line stretched next to the kitchen, and Adam helped serve the portions of bread and soup.

Chapter 6

The morning light woke them.

"Our mothers didn't come to get us," said Thomas, still drowsy.

"They'll come, but till they do, we have to fix up the nest. Did you sleep well?"

"I usually sleep deeply, but last night I couldn't sleep. Too many pictures raced before my eyes."

"I'm not worried. My mom is stubborn. She keeps her promises," said Adam.

"My mom is also stubborn and keeps her promises. But why didn't she come and get us?"

"I think we shouldn't worry. Worry won't do us any good." Adam spoke in a practical tone.

"I had a strange dream," said Thomas. "It was summer. We were swimming in the river. The sun was bright and pleasant. Then suddenly, without warning, black clouds gathered in the sky, and it started to rain hard. The light summer umbrellas were swept up by the wind and fell into the river. Dad suggested going up to the forest and looking for shelter there. We all made fun of his suggestion. 'It's a summer rainstorm, a passing shower, soon the sun will come out again. There's no reason to hurry.' Dad was insulted by our mockery, and his spirits fell. A strange dream. They say dreams come to teach us something." Thomas spoke excitedly.

"I don't have dreams. Only very rarely." Adam spoke lightly.

"I dream often, but usually I can't understand the dream. Sometimes the dream seems real, and sometimes it's confusion."

Adam raised his eyes with a faraway look as if he was still attached to his mother and to his schoolbooks.

Thomas was surprised by Adam's look and said, "Did I say something wrong?"

"No, Thomas. Everything is fine."

"What are you thinking about?"

"About our nest. We can improve it. We'll add twigs and leaves. A nest has to be well cushioned, otherwise it will cave in under our weight."

Strange, Adam isn't worried. The thought flashed through Thomas's mind. *Maybe he knows something that I don't. He's quick. He's a child of nature. I'm a city creature.*

They came down from the tree, washed their faces, drank some water, and looked around. Not a sound could be heard. The forest was covered with delicate points of light, blinking and shimmering.

"Come, let's have a little meal next to the stream. We still have some sandwiches, vegetables, and fruit," Adam suggested.

"Excellent idea. I'm hungry."

Adam climbed up and helped Thomas up, and soon they had sandwiches, fruit, and vegetables. Thomas's mood improved from minute to minute. Adam gave him a friendly look and said, "The forest is the safest place these days. In the ghetto they snatch up children and grandparents. Here they won't catch us. We'll improve our running and tree climbing, and we'll leap like squirrels."

"Maybe because I'm nearsighted, and maybe for other reasons, I'm not quick. My running isn't graceful." Thomas lost his self-confidence.

"You mustn't lose hope, Thomas. If you keep practicing, you'll get better at it."

"Are we going to stay in the forest for a long time?" Thomas asked.

"As long as we have to, until the ghetto calms

down. Maybe the war will be over in the mean-time."

"I'm afraid," Thomas admitted. "Why am I always afraid?"

"There's nothing to be afraid of. The forest has everything. We'll learn how to find the good things in the forest. Yesterday we took the first important step. We built a nest."

"You say that building the nest was the first step?" Thomas asked.

"That's right," said Adam. "When you have a base, you can move forward."

"Adam, your way of thinking surprises me."

Chapter 7

They went out to look for berries.

"It's great to eat berries that you picked your-self," said Adam.

They didn't have to go far. Right nearby there was a clearing full of little wild strawberries. First they picked and ate them. Then they took hand-fuls and went back to sit under the tree.

"What luck," said Thomas.

"My mom says that God provides food for every creature," said Adam.

"Is your family religious?"

"We go to synagogue on the holidays."

"Is a religious person different from a regular one?" Thomas asked.

"I don't think so," Adam answered. "My grandpa

says everyone was created in the image of God."

"Can you see God?" Thomas persisted.

"You're not allowed to see God. You have to do what pleases him."

"What pleases him?"

"To love your parents. To love your grandparents and people who need help."

"You surprise me, Adam."

"How?"

"I didn't imagine that you went to synagogue. I was sure that only old people went to synagogue."

They picked some more berries, and Thomas remembered painfully that his mother had promised to come to the forest and get him.

"Our mothers are doing what they can. They're probably busy hiding our grandparents," said Adam.

"True. I have to get over my egotism," said Thomas.

"Forgive my ignorance. What's 'egotism'?" Adam said.

"Loving yourself too much."

"Thomas, you know a lot. You won't only be the best in our class, but the best in the school."

"My father's the best, not me," said Thomas, sidestepping the praise Adam showered on him.

"Let's do something useful. Let's gather branches

and fix up the nest."

They gathered branches of various sizes. Adam climbed up into the tree, and Thomas handed him what they had collected. Adam spread out the branches and leaves and finally spread a blanket over them.

"Thomas. You won't recognize our nest. Tonight we'll sleep like kings," said Adam from above.

Thomas climbed up carefully and right away he saw: wider, more stable, and pleasant to lie on. They both lay down and stretched out their legs, pleased at the thickness of the nest.

"We've hardly been here for a day and a half, and it seems as if we've been here for a long time. Do you have the same feeling?" Thomas asked.

"I don't think about my feelings."

"You're lucky," said Thomas.

"Why?"

"Sometimes feelings are oppressive," Thomas told him.

While they were talking, they saw a white dog in the distance, borne lightly on long legs. "Hey, beautiful dog," Adam called out, but the dog didn't stop; it disappeared.

When he was younger, Thomas wanted to adopt a dog, but his mother refused absolutely.

That refusal made his childhood miserable, and every time he went outdoors and saw a puppy, his heart would go out to it. Once he found a puppy in the yard, and after he played with it, he brought it home. When his mother saw the puppy held against his chest, she screamed. Thomas dropped the puppy, but his mother kept screaming, and the puppy ran for its life.

That night, before he went to sleep, after she had read a fairy tale to him, his mother looked at him and said, "I want to apologize."

"For what, Mom?"

"For not letting you adopt a dog. It's my fault. When I was a little girl, about your age, there was a sweet puppy in the neighborhood where I grew up, and everybody played with it. One morning the rumor spread that the sweet puppy was infected with rabies, and we were all taken to the hospital for injections. I swore to myself that I'd never touch a dog again. When I saw the puppy up against your chest, I got very frightened. I shouldn't have screamed so loudly and frightened you. Forgive me, Thomas. I don't know if you can forgive me now, but I hope that one day you will," she said and burst into tears.

"Mom, I forgive you now."

"Thank you. It's been bothering me all day long."

Now Thomas saw his mother very clearly, sitting next to him. It seemed as if she were still tormenting herself because she had screamed, and Thomas wanted to repeat, "I forgive you with all my heart."

"Thomas, don't forgive me so easily. I don't deserve it," she said and disappeared from his sight.

For a long time he expected to see her face again, but it didn't return.

Chapter 8

"What are you thinking about, Thomas?" Adam asked cautiously.

"About my mom."

"Did she speak to you?"

"Yes, but it's complicated. It's hard to talk about now. I'll tell you some other time."

"There's time," said Adam calmly.

"Will we stay here for many days?" Thomas was afraid.

"I don't know. My grandpa says, 'It's in the hands of heaven.'"

"I never heard that expression. My dad says: 'Everything is in man's hands,'" said Thomas.

"Every house has its own expressions," said Adam. "Hasn't the time come to trade sandwiches? I'll give you mine, and you can give me yours." Thomas spoke in a lively way.

"Good idea," said Adam.

"The school year is nearly over. It's two o'clock, and everybody is going home. Just we two are out in nature. Do you understand what's happening to us?" Thomas spoke with concern.

"It's very simple. We're in hiding."

"You call the place where we are 'hiding'?" asked Thomas, emphasizing every word.

"I can't think of a better name. Our hiding place is big. You can walk around in it, climb trees, and drink water from the stream, but it's still a hiding place."

"I have the feeling that since the ghetto, nothing makes sense. They send away the old people. Why are they sending away the old people? Why are they sending away children? What harm did the children do? What harm did the old people do?" Thomas spoke emotionally.

"They're Jews," Adam answered quietly.

"Because they're Jews, they have to be sent away?"

"You know, Thomas. People don't like Jews."

"I can't figure that out. Apparently I have to experience and learn more," said Thomas, and then he stopped talking. He took a bite of Adam's sandwich and said, "Your sandwich is very tasty. It has black olives."

Then they climbed down and drank from the stream, picked berries, and remembered the tall, white dog that had run quickly through the forest and disappeared.

"Will it come back?" Thomas wondered.

"I assume so." Adam used an expression that Thomas used often.

Then, without advance notice, Thomas closed his eyes, curled up, and fell asleep.

Adam watched him in his sleep and was surprised by the speed with which Thomas had passed from the world of wakefulness to the world of slumber. Adam wasn't idle. He went out to see what else grew in the forest. He didn't have to go far. Right next to them a cherry tree grew, and it was full of dark fruit. At first he wanted to wake up Thomas and show him the tree, but when he went back and saw how deep his sleep was, he let him be. He went back to the cherry tree, picked a handful, and returned to Thomas, amazed how well he was sleeping.

Chapter 9

Thomas awoke in alarm.

"What's the matter, Thomas?" Adam came to him. "I was late for school."

"You had a bad dream. We don't go to school anymore. We live in the forest."

Adam showed him the cherries, and Thomas was enthusiastic. "What great cherries." They sat and ate, enjoying the sweet taste of the black fruit.

"Where did you find the cherry tree?"

"Right nearby."

"Adam, you have an unusual ability to discover things."

"I love to find new things."

"New things don't come to me, because I'm nearsighted."

You know how to sleep and dream, Adam wanted to say, but he didn't, to avoid hurting his feelings.

Adam noticed that Thomas had stopped asking why his mother was late, but when evening fell, Thomas said softly, "Now the pupils in our class are at home doing homework. Only we two are abandoned in the forest."

Adam sensed that the word "abandoned" was dripping with sorrow and yearning, so he asked, "Why did you say 'abandoned'?"

"What should I have said? Do you have a better word?"

"We have been sent to learn directly from nature and to grow up."

"Did our mothers bring us to the forest so we'd grow up?" asked Thomas in a tone that embarrassed Adam slightly.

"That idea just occurred to me now," said Adam, laughing.

"As far as I know, you don't start growing up at the age of nine," said Thomas.

Then they went up to the nest.

"Our nest is well cushioned," said Adam.

"True. It makes you want to sleep," Thomas agreed.

The forest air and fatigue wrapped around the two boys, and they fell asleep.

Thomas dreamed that his mother was sitting

on his bed and reading to him from *Demian*, a book by Hermann Hesse. His mother's voice, before he fell asleep, was soft and calm, and the story appealed to him. Suddenly Thomas thought to ask his mother, "Why did you send me to the forest? Did you send me so I would grow up?" His mother was upset by his question. "I had no choice. I was afraid they would snatch you up." "Where are they sending the children and the old people?" "Why do you ask?" "There are various rumors. When will the war be over?" "I don't know. The moment it's over, I'll come and get you. You have to be patient."

Thomas woke up very early, before sunrise. Adam was still asleep. The clear dream became even brighter, and he saw his mother before his eyes.

Adam woke up and asked, "Why aren't you asleep?"

"I had a dream, and I guess it woke me up."

"A good dream?"

"Mom promised she'll come as soon as the war is over," Thomas told him.

"When will the war be over?" Adam asked.

"She didn't tell me in so many words. Dreams always hint, but they never explain."

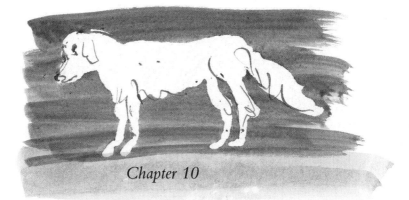

Chapter 10

When they came down from the nest, a surprise awaited them. The white dog was standing near them on his tall, thin legs. Adam was glad and knelt down right away, stroking him and asking, "What's your name, nice dog? My name is Adam, and I'm in the forest with my friend Thomas. I have a dog that I love in town. He's smaller than you, and his name is Miro."

The dog was astonished by Adam's words and petting, and he stood still. It was hard to say whether he was a pet dog or a stray. His fur was smooth, and he wasn't neglected. If he wasn't neglected, that was a sign he was a pet. He has had enough to eat, the thought flashed through Adam's mind.

Adam kept talking to him. He asked about his home, but because the dog didn't respond, he asked, "Maybe you're looking for a friend?"

He didn't respond to that question either. He became more and more mute, and Adam realized that the dog didn't understand human language. The people he lived with didn't talk to him and weren't interested in him.

Thomas, who was standing at the side all the time, didn't join in Adam's efforts to get that pretty, thin creature to talk. He asked bashfully, "Can I touch him?"

"Of course. He came to visit both of us."

Thomas drew close to the dog, stroked him, and said, "My name is Thomas." Then he withdrew, pleased he had overcome his fear.

"Talk to him some more," Adam encouraged him.

"What should I say to him?"

"Ask him where he came to us from."

"It's hard for me to talk to him. I'm not used to talking to dogs."

"In a day or two you'll learn how to talk to animals. It's not hard."

Adam patted the dog again. Filled with pleasure and trust, the dog sat down and closed its eyes.

"We're going to be good friends," Adam said, hugging the dog. The dog shook himself and stood up. Adam kept trying to talk him into staying. "We'll love you and treat you well."

The dog looked at him with his big eyes, and it was evident that his patience was wearing out. Adam took a sugar cube out of his pocket and brought it to the dog's mouth. The dog smelled it and swallowed the sugar. Thomas and Adam stood tensely and watched the dog's expressions. The dog stood there for a while and finally slipped out of Adam's arms and went on his way.

Adam wanted to run after him, but when he saw that the dog was running hard, he called out, "Don't forget to come back to visit us. We're expecting you." He waited for the dog to turn his head back to him, but when he didn't, Adam stood still and followed him with his eyes as he went away.

The dog apparently knew its way and disappeared. Adam stood still, stunned.

"What's the matter, Adam?" Thomas was alarmed.

"The dog left part of himself with us," said Adam.

"I don't understand you, Adam. You have to explain to me."

"When animals go away, they leave part of themselves with you."

"Do you really feel it, or are you imagining it?"
"I feel it in my hand or my knees, and sometimes in my whole body."

"Strange," said Thomas. "Anyway, you spoke to the dog in a very natural way. How did you learn how to talk to dogs?"

"From Miro, our dog."

"Do you talk to him the way you talked to the dog that came to visit us?"

"I talk to Miro like a friend."

"Do you understand him, or does it just seem like it?"

"I understand him, and he understands me." Adam didn't get confused.

"Still, dogs aren't in the human family." Thomas spoke in his father's voice.

"Miro is part of our family. Mom and Dad understand him even better than I do."

"Strange."

"What's so strange?"

"I guess I'll never know how to talk to a dog."

"Don't worry, Thomas. The forest will teach you."

When he heard Adam's words, Thomas smiled and was about to say, Can you learn everything? Some people learn arithmetic easily, and some people learn how to draw easily. Not everyone knows how to learn everything. But for some reason he stopped himself and didn't say it.

Light filled the forest. From a distance, mooing, the neighing of horses, and barking could be heard. The sounds reminded Adam of the long excursions he had made with his parents in the Carpathian Mountains, the low wooden houses, the green meadows spotted with cows, sheep, and horses. At noon they used to enter a roadside tavern, order a corn pudding filled with cherries. For dessert—a cup of ice cream.

Thomas dreamed a strange dream that night. He and his mother were standing at the door of their house. Suddenly his father appeared from a side entrance, and he was short and skinny. His back was bent. It was hard to recognize him.

"What happened?" his mother called out in surprise.

When he heard her voice, his father's face beamed, and he said, "They made us work and starved us from morning to night, but they didn't break our spirits. We studied whenever we could. I taught a class in history, and my friend Herman taught one in literature. We didn't have books, but our memories didn't betray us."

While he was talking, he collapsed and passed out. Thomas and his mother ran over to him, knelt down, and poured water on his face.

Chapter 11

That same morning, a squirrel came to visit them. Adam knelt and asked, "How are you, squirrel?" The squirrel hopped and raised its body upright. Its chatter said, You're new in the forest, aren't you?

Adam offered it pieces of the sandwich he was eating. The squirrel was cautious, sniffed, tasted, hopped away, and kept nibbling at the bread.

After finishing the crumbs, the squirrel moved away, bowed once to the right and once to the left, and returned to its tree.

"I noticed," said Thomas, "that some of the squirrel's movements are like people's. Am I mistaken?"

"You're not mistaken. We have more in common with animals than we have differences," said Adam, pleased with his own words.

"Anyway, you talked to the squirrel the way one person talks to his fellow," said Thomas.

Adam chuckled. "I've never heard a child say 'the way one person talks to his fellow.'"

"My parents say 'the way one person talks to his fellow.' Is that incorrect?" Thomas asked.

They ate breakfast and for dessert they ate some of the cherries they had set aside for a long day full of sun.

"Isn't it strange that we're living in the forest without parents and without friends? What harm did we do? I have the feeling that it's a punishment. It's not clear to me who's punishing us, or for what." Thomas spoke quickly, without stopping between the words.

"We're Jews," said Adam, as though it were self-evident.

"What harm did the Jews do to deserve punishment?" Thomas didn't let up.

"People don't like Jews."

"Are we different from other people?" Thomas was puzzled.

"Apparently."

"I don't see any difference between Jews and non-Jews," Thomas insisted.

Adam got impatient, and he said, "The Jews have always suffered."

"Why?"

"It's a riddle," said Adam, surprising Thomas.

"There have to be reasons." Thomas spoke like his father, the teacher.

"We won't solve that problem today." Adam also spoke like *his* father. "Let's take a look around the forest. I know it well. Sitting for too long gives you bad thoughts."

"Shouldn't I think?" Thomas jumped up.

"You don't have to think all the time."

"My father wouldn't agree with that," said Thomas.

While they were walking around, wonders appeared before their eyes. First they met a lilac bush in full bloom with its violet flowers. Adam walked up to the bush, picked a small branch, and put it to his nose. "A marvelous smell, like the bush we have in our garden."

"I thought that lilacs only grew in gardens," Thomas commented.

"Lilacs grow in well-lit places in the forest," said Adam, glad to have remembered his mother's words.

Thomas turned his face toward him. Again he was surprised by Adam's capability.

Not far from the lilacs a wild rose bush grew.

"The forest isn't monotonous," said Thomas in a grown-up way.

They went in deeper and saw more wonders. Suddenly Thomas was frightened and said, "I think something happened to Mom. There's a reason why she didn't come on time. Can we go back to our tree now? Is it far?"

"It's not far. We'll be next to it in ten minutes," Adam reassured him.

So it was. In a few minutes they were standing next to their tree, and Thomas was relieved.

Chapter 12

But the night was not quiet. First they heard the footsteps of someone fleeing, then shots echoed. Adam and Thomas lay tensely in the nest and listened.

After midnight there was silence, but Adam and Thomas didn't stick their heads out of the nest. They kept listening, and Adam said, "We'll have to find ourselves a more secure hideout. Deeper in the forest the foliage is thicker."

"I feel bad about our nest," said Thomas.

"The nest we'll build will be better."

"When will we move out?"

"Before sunrise. But first let's eat something. My sandwich is very good."

"Mine, too. Too bad it's our last sandwich. We weren't provident."

"Being provident wouldn't have helped us. In a couple of days we'd have finished the last sandwich."

"You're right," Thomas agreed.

They sat for a while, silent and listening intently. Finally Adam said, "Let's go down," and he quickly slid down the tree. Thomas threw down the two backpacks and the blankets, and Adam helped Thomas come down the tree.

After an hour of pushing through the thick underbrush, they stopped and stood next to a tree whose top was like the one where they had built their nest.

"Hooray, Adam. This is a splendid tree," said Thomas as he took off his backpack.

"Once I went by this tree with Mom and Dad. Even then it made an impression on me. I didn't imagine that it would be our new nest," said Adam.

Without delay they started breaking off branches and twigs and collecting them. Adam climbed up to the treetop, and Thomas handed him the branches and twigs they had gathered. They found that the new treetop was thicker and wider than the other one. Adam, who was experienced in nest building by now, did it quickly this time.

Thomas asked, "More branches?"

"A few more."

Then they took the backpacks up. Thomas climbed up and got scratched.

"Don't worry, Thomas. I have a bandage and iodine in my backpack."

The wound was bleeding, but Thomas didn't complain.

"You did everything like an experienced forester," Adam said as he bandaged Thomas's arm. "Now you'll have a scar, and it will show that you climbed tall trees."

The first lights shone on the treetops, but Adam and Thomas were in no hurry to go down. They surveyed the forest and listened to the noises.

"How's your wound, Thomas?"

"It hurts, but it's not too bad."

They crouched and kept looking and listening. There were still some candies in Thomas's backpack. They sucked them and quieted their hunger. Around noontime, when their hunger increased, they slid down the tree and started searching.

They didn't find any water, but they did find a berry patch and started picking right away. The berries were small and particularly tasty.

They sat at the foot of a tree and looked around.

Suddenly Adam knelt down, put his ear to the ground, and called out loud, "I hear the murmuring of water."

They made a trail and stopped to listen from time to time. In a little while they found a flowing stream.

Thus another day passed. Thomas was less worried. They both were busy improving the nest and finding raspberries and blueberries, and going back to the cherry tree. They even found an apple tree. The apples were sour, but they weren't tasteless.

But hunger didn't stop plaguing them. They yearned for bread and soup, for all the foods their mothers made. Adam, who usually didn't dream, dreamed that his mother was standing in the kitchen and making a sandwich for him. "I was so hungry that I grabbed the sandwich from Mom's hands. Suddenly I was ashamed and begged her pardon. Mom wasn't angry. She looked at me with tears in her eyes and said, 'No wonder you're hungry.' I bit into the sandwich and ate it with an appetite. In my dream I ate a whole sandwich, but now I'm hungry," Adam said, laughing.

Thomas was so hungry he was dreaming while awake. He muttered and put his hand over his eyes as if he was dazzled.

"What do you see, Thomas?" Adam asked.

"I see Mom carrying a big tray of food in a pot."

"Is she coming close to you?"

"She comes close and moves away and makes me dizzy."

"I'd suggest that you take your hands away from your eyes."

"I'll fall down."

"Let's eat some cherries."

"I'm afraid. The cherries will give me diarrhea."

"So come and drink some water. Water never does any harm."

Thomas took his hands away from his eyes and said, "Sorry, Adam. Hunger is deceiving me, and I have a stomachache."

"Thomas, don't worry. We'll do whatever is possible and even the impossible, and we'll produce bread from the earth," said Adam, and for a moment he managed to make Thomas laugh.

The nights were cold, and two sweaters and coats didn't keep them warm enough. In Adam's opinion they had no alternative but to go deeper into the forest. "That's the only place where we'll be able to light a campfire and get warm," he said.

Thomas observed Adam, listened to him, and

repeated to himself, Adam has practical sense. He's an excellent guide.

While they were on their way to the stream to wash their faces and drink, Adam spied an old peasant sheepskin cloak in the distance. He went over and picked it up. The coat was old and worn, but it was still in one piece.

"It's a miracle," Adam called out.

"Finding an old cloak is a miracle?" Thomas wondered.

"There's no other word for it," said Adam. "In any case, somebody is thinking about us."

"Do you mean that God is thinking about us?"

"I guess so," said Adam, stunning Thomas even more.

That night rain fell. But Adam and Thomas didn't get wet. The raindrops rolled off the coat they had found.

"We're lucky," said Thomas.

Adam wanted to say, It isn't a matter of luck, but he wasn't sure whether it was right to say that.

Toward the end of the night they heard the footsteps of someone running away, but there were no shots. "We can't keep hiding this way, when people are in danger," said Adam. "We'll have to go down and help."

"How can we help?" asked Thomas.

"We can prepare a thermos bottle of water, iodine, and some fruit. If we see someone trip and fall, we can go down and help him."

This time Thomas wasn't put off by the new task. He said, "Studying is important, but helping people in trouble is more important."

Adam listened carefully to the sentence that Thomas spoke, and he knew: Thomas was trying with all his might. In a little while he'd overcome his fear.

Chapter 13

The surprises came one after the other. They kept on exploring the forest and found a small pool full of water plants. "This is where the frogs we hear at night live," said Adam excitedly.

Adam was happy every time they discovered something. Thomas was still reserved. Still fearful. In the depth of his heart he was still thinking about his parents and his house, and when he didn't think about them, dreams came at night and showed them to him.

Nevertheless Thomas wasn't the same Thomas whom Adam had first met in the forest. He was still fearful. But he climbed the tree without help. Also, when he climbed down from the tree, he did it more steadily.

They ate raspberries and blueberries as well as an apple or two, but that good fruit wasn't filling.

Hunger made them dizzy. They sat next to the stream, and from time to time they'd drink some water.

Are we going to die of hunger? Thomas's eyes asked.

Adam looked at him with friendship and said, "The forest has a lot more gifts to make us happy. Gradually we'll discover them. If we're alert and diligent, we'll find them. Just a few days ago we found a cloak to protect us."

But what will happen in the meantime, until we find the gifts? Thomas's eyes asked once again.

"Thomas, we have to get used to the food of the forest. True, it's different from the food we had at home, it's not easy to get used to new food, but we'll do it."

"You're a boy who believes," Thomas surprised Adam. "You don't get discouraged easily. I keep asking myself: Why am I here? Why have I been punished? That's probably wrong of me."

"You can correct mistakes. If we don't think about the past, but if we think about what we have to do, our mood will improve."

Thomas listened carefully to Adam's words and asked, "Who did you learn that practical way of thinking from?"

"From Mom and Dad. I also love to hear my grandparents. They always tell me useful things. When I'm sad, Grandma tells me: 'Things to make you happy will come your way. You mustn't be too sad. You have to accept what's good and what's not so good, because everything comes from God.'"

Thomas meant to ask how we can know that everything comes from God, but hunger made him tired, and he fell asleep.

That night Thomas awoke from a bad dream and sat up, stunned.

"What's the matter, Thomas?" Adam asked gently. "I had a bad dream, and it's hard for me to shake it off."

"What did you see? Tell me." "I'm hesitant to tell you."

"Was it a clear dream, or a mixed-up one?" "It was a clear dream, but painful."

"Tell me. You'll feel better."

"I dreamed I was in school, during recess. Suddenly the children stood up and told me I was going to be punished. 'Why? What harm did I do?' I asked, and my body was trembling. Everybody fixed me with their eyes and said, 'We're tired of you. Your constant excellence not only makes us angry, it's unbearable.' 'I'm prepared to give up the excellence,' I told them. 'You already promised that once,' the main bully said. 'We don't believe you anymore.' 'What can I do to make you believe me?' 'We decided to whip you. Lie down on that chair.' 'If you want to hit me, hit me, but I won't lie on that chair.' Hearing my words, they all burst out in hard laughter and slipped their leather belts from their pants. They whipped me hard, and it was painful. It's a good thing I woke up."

"Thomas, you had a very bad dream," said Adam, "but you resisted like a hero."

"I was trembling," Thomas admitted.

"In that situation, one against many, anyone, not just a boy, would have trembled. It's important to say that you resisted like a hero and didn't give in. Bravo. After a dream like that you deserve a good breakfast."

When he heard Adam's words, Thomas's eyes filled with tears.

Chapter 14

After eating raspberries and blueberries, they went out to explore the forest. Hunger was weakening them. After a short walk, they stopped and sat down. Thomas sank into reverie.

"A penny for your thoughts, Thomas," said Adam. "I was thinking about the dream I had. It won't let go of me."

"Thomas, in that dream you were a guy who didn't give in. Sure, you got whipped, but you didn't surrender. You can be proud of yourself."

While they were walking, dizzy with hunger, before their eyes, between the trees, lay a meadow with a cow and a calf. The cow didn't seem to be used to strangers, and she was surprised. But the calf wasn't frightened. It looked at them with eyes full of wonder. The meadow was fenced in. After looking at it from all sides, Adam entered, patted the cow and the calf, and, without delay, started to milk the cow. He caught the milk in his cupped hand and drank. Right away he invited Thomas to join him in drinking. They drank the fresh milk sip by sip. If they had had a cup or bowl, they could have milked some more. But they were happy with what the morning had given them and withdrew into the forest.

"There's nothing like fresh milk," said Adam.

"I forgot. I have a thermos bottle in my pack. Let's bring it and fill it with milk," said Thomas.

They didn't hurry back. They looked around to see whether there were any suspicious creatures, and only after making certain there was no danger, they returned to their tree. Thomas climbed up to the nest and brought down the thermos bottle. They hurried back to the meadow.

Adam milked the cow and filled the thermos bottle. If they hadn't been afraid of the owner of the cow and the calf, they would have stayed and petted the dear creatures they had found.

They went back to the tree, climbed up, and sipped the milk. With every sip, they felt the fresh milk slaking their thirst and satisfying their hunger. Without noticing, they fell asleep.

When they woke up, toward evening, Thomas said, "I dreamed a strange dream. A white dream. Everything looked white: the trees, the streets, and the people."

"Were the people in a panic?" Adam asked.

"No, everyone was standing there, bewildered."

"And were you white, too?"

"I was apparently whiter than everyone. They all looked at me, and they were sure I was the one who had brought about that whitening."

"What did you say to them?"

"I didn't know what to say."

"You had that white dream because we drank that good, fresh milk. Grandma says, 'A white dream is a good dream,'" said Adam.

"Thanks for interpreting the dream," said Thomas.

Crouching and with caution, they went back to visit the cow and her calf. When they were close they saw that the grass was still there, but the cow and the calf were gone.

Adam didn't look worried. "The forest has a lot more presents for us."

"I see that you trust the forest," said Thomas.

"The forest is sometimes better than people," said Adam.

Thomas commented, "The forest always appears to us as a place where wild animals live."

"Don't forget. Wild animals only attack when they're hungry."

"That shows that people are worse than them," said Thomas, speaking in his father's words.

Chapter 15

The next day, when they went to see the cow and her calf, they found a little girl, dressed in peasant clothes, milking the cow. They clung to one of the trees and stared at her tensely.

"She's very short, but she's sweet," said Thomas.

Adam, who had concentrated on her face and hands as she milked, discovered she was Mina, a girl from their class.

Adam didn't restrain himself but called out in a whisper, "Mina."

The girl didn't respond to his call.

"Are you sure it's Mina?" Thomas asked fearfully. "I have no doubt."

"Mina. It's Adam and Thomas. We live in the forest and we're eating berries. If you could bring us some bread, we'd be very grateful," Adam said to her.

She didn't respond to that call either. She kept milking. When the bucket was full, she quickly took it and the stool she had been sitting on and disappeared between the trees.

"It's Mina, without doubt," Adam murmured. "She has changed a bit, but her expression hasn't changed."

"How did you recognize her?"

"I sat next to her in second grade. I remember the way she sat and the expression of her face."

"Strange. In the spring we were still in school, and now we're all on our own," Thomas said to himself.

Indeed Mina was short and skinny, and she didn't stand out in the class. She did all her homework seriously and diligently, but she didn't attract attention or affection. They didn't assign her tasks. She didn't play in the school yard, and she didn't have friends. At the time of the ghetto, she worked in the hospital with her mother. She helped wash and feed the patients. The patients were fond of her and called her the little angel. Mina floated from room to room. She brought medicine to this one and a bowl of soup to that one. After a while people heard that her mother had found a pair of peasants who were willing to hide her for money.

"That's Mina. I'm sure," Adam muttered again.

They were sitting near the brook, looking at the shimmering water in silence.

"The brook is a living thing," said Adam. "Do you mean that the brook gives us life?"

"Not exactly. It's good to observe its shining motion. Your eyes love to look at water, and it gives the heart joy."

"Strange," said Thomas. "What's so strange?"

"We have to learn from everything, my father says. What can be learned from water?"

"It's hard for me to explain. If it makes you happy to look at the flowing water, it will make you happy to look at a sleeping dog," said Adam, and they both laughed.

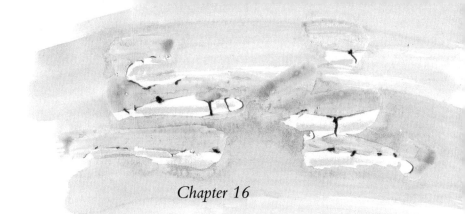

Chapter 16

After that Adam began to steal in and milk the cow. The fresh milk nourished them. Every day they practiced running in a crouch, finding hiding places, and climbing trees. Thomas was glad to be running with Adam. If they hadn't been weak, they would have exercised more. The raspberries and blueberries and the bit of milk did nourish them, but not enough. "Bread, bread," Thomas called out from time to time, and they both laughed.

They saw Mina milking the cow again. Adam called to her in a whisper, "Mina, Adam and Thomas are here. If you bring us some bread, we'll be very grateful."

Mina didn't respond.

Mina's father died when she was five, and her mother worked as a housekeeper. They were poor, but her mother made sure that poverty didn't shame them. She dressed Mina in nice clothes and bought her notebooks and textbooks.

"Are you certain it's Mina?" Thomas asked repeatedly.

"I'm 100 percent sure."

Still wondering how they could get solid food, they returned to the meadow and hid behind a tree near the edge to get as close as they could to Mina. Then they looked down and found half a loaf of bread and a piece of cheese wrapped in an old newspaper.

"I wasn't wrong," Adam called out.

They sat down by the brook. Adam cut a slice of bread and a piece of cheese for each of them with his jackknife, and they could barely believe their eyes.

They wanted to rejoice, but they were afraid. The long days of hunger had weakened them. The fresh bread they gobbled down stuck between their throats and their stomachs and hurt them.

"In the future we'll eat more slowly," said Thomas.

They drank water from the brook. The water washed down the bread, and the pain passed.

"Someone is watching over us," said Adam. "Do you mean that God is watching over us?" Adam was silent. Tears filled his eyes.

The next evening, when Mina came to milk the cow, Adam approached the tree closest to her and called out in a whisper, "Thank you, Mina. We hadn't eaten bread for many days."

This time, too, Mina didn't respond. After she finished milking, she took the stool and the pail and disappeared.

Adam and Thomas watched her in amazement. She had changed in a short time. She hadn't grown taller, but her face and her body were fuller. When she milked, she looked like a peasant girl.

"Those changes didn't come easily to her," said Adam.

"How do you know?"

"Changing isn't a simple matter. It takes determination. You have to alter all the movements your body is used to. You have to block your thoughts and speak in a language that isn't yours. Lucky for us we're in the forest and not with Diana, where we were supposed to hide, or who knows where. At Diana's we would have been different creatures, swineherds, or who knows what. We're suffering from hunger, but we're still who we were. We have the forest and the brook, and we're speaking the language we're used to." Adam spoke at length and with emotion.

"Mina has changed, but apparently not in her soul. She took the risk of bringing us bread. You have to admire her courage," said Thomas.

"That's true. If it sounded like I was looking down on her for changing, I apologize," said Adam.

Every few days she left them a hunk of bread or a piece of corn pie. Once she left them a big red tomato.

"God sent Mina to us to rescue us from hunger," said Adam.

"Does the messenger know she's a messenger, or does she do it without knowing?" Thomas spoke in his father's words.

"You're great at phrasing things," said Adam.

"I have to be careful. Sometimes Mom and Dad speak from my mouth," said Thomas, laughing.

Chapter 17

In the middle of the night, while they were wondering what they could do and where they could turn and how they could get another coat or a blanket to warm the nest, they heard a moan of pain. Adam and Thomas quickly climbed down from the tree and ran toward the sound of the groaning. Not far from the tree lay a man, breathing heavily.

Adam leaned over the man on the ground and said, "My name is Adam. Where does it hurt?"

"I'm weak. They've been running after me for two days. I'm exhausted."

"We have a little fresh milk and some bread."

"I'm thirsty. If you have water, that will save me."

"Drink some milk, and later we'll bring you water."

The two boys lifted the man's head, and he

took a sip and then another. "Now we'll go and fetch you some water.

"Thanks, boys, thanks, angels."

They raced to the stream, rinsed out the thermos and filled it with water. The man drank and drank. He opened his eyes and said, "Angel children. Where are you from? Who sent you to save me?"

"My name is Adam, and my friend's name is Thomas. We've been hiding in the forest since the beginning of the summer."

"Did you hear my voice?"

"We heard it clearly. We have a nest in the top of a tall tree. You can hear things well from there. How are the people in the ghetto?"

"The ghetto has been liquidated."

"Where were the people sent?"

"To Poland."

"Have they gotten there?" Thomas asked cautiously.

"I assume so."

While they were talking, they heard shots. The man raised his head and called out, "Run away, boys. I'll look for a hiding place." When Adam and Thomas didn't move, he called out, "Quickly, quickly. You can't stay near me."

They returned to the tree in a crouch. The

shooting continued, but they were glad they had managed to help the man who was running away. They were still worried about him. Who knew whether he had found a hiding place, whether he would hold out. They forgot about their own concerns. The image of the fugitive didn't leave their sight.

With the last darkness the shooting subsided. They were in no hurry to come down. They listened. They didn't leave the tree until first light. They trotted to the stream in a crouch, washed their faces, and drank.

They still had bread and some cheese.

"Adam, do you believe that God will reveal himself to us soon?" Thomas asked.

"I don't expect so. I expect my mom and dad to return to me," Adam surprised him.

"I thought that a believer would expect God to reveal himself."

"Grandfather says, 'God dwells everywhere.' Whoever looks for God can find him any-where—with people, with animals, and even in some inanimate things."

"Does God also dwell in evil people?"

"Evil people have driven him out of them-selves."

"I didn't know," said Thomas. "Does your grandfather speak to you sometimes?"

"Grandfather isn't talkative. He's the silent type."

～

While they were wondering what to do and where to go, they saw a dog in the distance, sniffing intently, going from tree to tree and sticking his nose among the bushes. Suddenly he raised his head and started running toward them.

It was Miro, Miro and none other.

Adam knelt, spread his arms, hugged Miro, and his voice choked. Miro looked neglected. His fur was matted and his face was thin. Adam overcame his muteness and asked, "How did you find me?" He pressed his face against Miro's, kissed him, and pressed him to his chest.

Thomas was stunned. He had never seen such love for animals.

"This is my Miro, all mine." Adam pressed him against his body again. "He sleeps in my room and in the winter he curls up on my blanket. How could I live without you? How's Mom? How are my grandparents?" Miro let out a thin whine and shrank into Adam's arms.

Thomas roused himself from his amazement and asked, "How did he find you?"

"With Miro, anything is possible," Adam answered. "Did he ever find you before?"

"Mom once lost her wallet with money in it and was very upset. Miro saw she was upset and went out to look for the wallet, without anyone asking him to. Many hours passed, and he didn't come back. We were afraid something had happened to him. Later that evening he came back with the wallet in his mouth. Miro is a marvelous creature. Can't you see in him that he's marvelous?" Adam spoke excitedly.

Chapter 18

They couldn't believe how much their lives had changed. Adam washed Miro, filled his palm with water, and put it to his mouth. Miro was thirsty and drank till the last drop.

"Thomas and I live in the forest now. I haven't heard from Mom since we parted. I assume she's hiding along with my grandparents. You certainly know more than I do."

Miro looked at him with his big eyes, let out a few soft barks, and Adam sensed that Miro was moved by their meeting and it was hard for him to talk now.

Miro was a smart dog. He knew what was happening in the house, who was sad and who was sick. If one of Adam's grandparents were sick, he would sit by the bed and sympathize with his pain. On holidays he rejoiced with everyone.

"What happened to you, Miro, since I left you?" Thomas asked cautiously, "Can I pet Miro?"

"Certainly. Now he belongs to both of us." Thomas bent down on his knees and stroked Miro. Miro looked at him as if to say, I'm Adam's friend. I can't be your friend, too.

Even though Thomas didn't understand the language of animals, he understood that Miro was entirely devoted to Adam now. There was no room in his soul for another boy.

Adam noticed that Thomas's feelings were hurt, and he said, "Don't worry. He'll be your friend, too."

"I'm deaf and dumb with animals," said Thomas.

"You're wrong, Thomas. In a little while you'll be talking to him the way I do."

Adam carried Miro up into the nest, and that night all three of them slept there. They had a feeling that Miro brought a message from home with him. But for now he hadn't found the right little barks to express his message.

The next day Adam sensed that Miro was ready to tell him something. Miro raced from place to place restlessly, whining with little barks. Adam hugged him and whispered in his ears, "Tell me, dear, what you want to say to me. I'm listening."

At last Miro pulled at his collar with his hind leg again and again with nervous movements that Adam had never seen him make.

Adam took the collar off Miro's neck, and he found a letter folded up inside it.

Adam dear, pardon me. I couldn't come to you as I had promised. If you haven't gotten to Diana's yet, don't delay. Go to her. Give her the gold jewelry I sewed in your coat and tell her that I'll come soon and give her more. You know Diana. She's got a temper, but she's not a bad woman. I believe she'll hide you. But if for some reason she refuses to hide you, go to her cousin, Christina. She's a widow who lives near that poplar grove, and I'm sure she'll hide you.

I couldn't find a hiding place for your grandparents. I can't leave your grandparents on their own. Everyone says the war is nearly over. I pray that until then God will preserve you. You're a smart boy, and I count on your ability to make your way. Forgive your mother who loves you very much.

Adam read the letter again and again, and tears filled his eyes.

"What did your mother write to you?" Thomas approached Adam.

"Sorry, Thomas. It's hard for me to talk now," said Adam and pressed Miro against his body.

Chapter 19

The next day Adam milked the cow and filled the thermos bottle. They sat near the brook, and Miro joined in the meal. Miro didn't leave Adam's side. He brought little barks up from inside himself. They were familiar, but Adam couldn't decipher them. Adam knelt down and asked again, "What happened to Mom and my grandparents? When did they leave the house?"

Miro apparently knew a lot, too much to communicate what he knew to Adam with little barks. A day and a half had passed since his arrival, but he still hadn't calmed down.

Miro wasn't a big or purebred dog. He was black with white patches. He wasn't particularly handsome, but he was solidly built. His jumps were powerful, and he ran with long strides. He liked to be petted, but he didn't beg to be pampered, and he didn't annoy you by barking for no reason. Adam's father called him a "serious dog."

Adam kept rereading the letter that Miro had brought him. He felt the pain between the few sentences that his mother had written to him. His father was carrying iron tracks on his shoulder and collapsing under the weight of the burden. His mom and his grandparents were somewhere in Poland. Only a short time ago we were all together, and now everyone is somewhere else.

Thomas also thought about his father, who had been taken for forced labor, and about his mother, who was watching over the grandparents.

Suddenly Thomas turned to Adam and asked, "Is God watching over us?"

"Why do you ask?"

"Our situation worries me," said Thomas.

"My grandfathers are close to God. They pray to him and read holy books."

"Do you feel God?" Thomas surprised him.

"When I'm with my grandparents, I feel him."

"And you yourself, do you feel close to God?"

"Sometimes it seems like he is hovering above me," said Adam, and wonder filled his face.

Adam's answers didn't bring Thomas close to God. But Thomas felt that Adam wasn't making things up. He wasn't exaggerating. He was trying to convey his feelings.

"Adam, thanks for sharing your feelings with me."

"It's hard for me to talk about secret things. I don't have the right words," said Adam.

"I understand," said Thomas.

Mina hadn't forgotten them. Once again she left them a few pieces of corn pie and some cheese. She wrapped the package in newspaper and left it near the tree.

"If only it was possible to thank her," said Thomas.

"Nobody must see us with her. She's living a hidden life now," said Adam in a whisper.

"You're right," said Thomas, impressed by Adam's way of thinking.

That day Thomas managed to write in his diary:

Yesterday in a miraculous way Miro, Adam's dog, came to us. His surprising arrival strengthens my faith that the war is nearly over, and after it we'll meet. Miro is a wonderful creature. He wandered in the forest for many days before he found Adam. Adam found a letter from his mother in Miro's collar. His mother told him that she hadn't been able to find a hiding place for his grandparents, so all of them would go to the railroad station. Did you and my grandparents take the same path?

Until a short time ago forest fruit nourished us, but it's disappearing. Luckily for us we found a girl from our class, Mina, who's hiding with a peasant. She brings us bread or corn pie and cheese from time to time, and she's saving us from hunger.

Adam keeps saying: God sent Mina to us. It's hard for me to say a sentence like that. Adam comes from a religious family. Faith in God was planted in him. I can't forget what Dad always said, Human beings— only the good of human beings—is our concern. We don't deal in conjectures.

To tell the truth, Adam and I don't argue. We're busy from morning to night with strengthening the nest and getting food. It isn't easy to stay alive in the forest. Adam is a good friend and an optimistic boy. If it weren't for him, I doubt I would have lasted.

Chapter 20

Meanwhile it started to rain, heavy rain that forced them to go up into the nest and cover themselves with the shepherd's cloak. Miro was content. He clung to Adam, and for the first time he barked happily.

"It's a good thing we have the cloak to shield us. Miro will also protect us," said Adam.

The rain lasted all day and all night. The first time it stopped, they climbed down to see whether the cow and the calf were grazing in the field. They weren't there, but a small package, wrapped in a rag, was laying under the tree. There were a couple of slices of corn pie in it, a piece of cheese, and dried fruit.

Adam called out enthusiastically, "God sent us Mina."

"Adam, I'd like to believe in God, too."

"You have to be patient. Everyone comes to him in their own way."

"Dad says that faith in God has passed from the world," said Thomas.

"Thomas, your father is a man of integrity. He is devoted to his students heart and soul. He serves God in his own way."

"I guess I'll have to find my own way, too," said Thomas.

They climbed up to the nest and ate. Since Miro came, Thomas's mood changed. He no longer sank into sudden sadness. Miro seemed to feel affection for Thomas and let him pet him.

But the nights weren't peaceful. From time to time they heard the footsteps of someone running away, and sometimes they heard shots. From the distance heavy, dull noises could be heard, sounding like a mixture of lightning and thunder.

While they listened to the rain and the sound of explosions above them, once again they heard a man groaning in pain.

"Let's go down and see what happened," said Adam, immediately taking iodine and bandages from his backpack. Thomas took the thermos bottle with him and the remains of the corn pie.

Not far from the nest a man lay, tormented by pain. Adam recognized him right away: the music teacher.

"What happened, Mr. Braverman?" Adam leaned over him.

"Who are you?" he was roused from his pain.

"We're Adam and Thomas, your students."

"Sorry," he said, and his head sank to the ground.

"Are you wounded?" Adam whispered.

"In the leg."

"We have iodine and a bandage."

Adam rolled up his pant leg. He could see the blood and the wound despite the darkness.

"A bullet hit me, but it seems to have missed the bone."

After they washed the wounded area and put iodine on it, Mr. Braverman opened his eyes and said, "Thank you, boys." Miro kept walking around them, complaining because they weren't including him in the rescue.

When the first lights filtered into the forest, Mr. Braverman raised himself on his arms and said, "Thank you, boys, for your fine and devoted help. Now it's daytime, and you have to return to your hiding place."

"Please drink some water and have a bit of corn pie," Adam said.

The teacher sipped some water and tasted the

corn pie. Then he said, "Dear children, go back to where you were. We'll meet after the war."

"Is the war ending?" Thomas asked with a trembling voice.

"The German army is in retreat, and the Russian army is approaching. But for the Jews, there's no respite. They pursue every Jew who runs away. Where's your hiding place?"

"In the treetop."

"You're smart children. Don't go out in daylight."

"Where are you going, Mr. Braverman?"

"I'm going to look for my wife and children. If you run into them, tell them you saw me. I'll hide under a bush now, and at night I'll go on my way."

"If you meet our mothers, tell them we're in a safe place," Thomas said, overcoming his shyness.

"Of course. Hurry to your hiding place. You mustn't be out in daylight."

Everybody liked Mr. Braverman. He loved music, and he loved children. Everybody felt comfortable with him. He never failed a student. If somebody didn't have a good ear, he would say, "But your eyesight is probably better than ours. Nature compensates. Sometimes nature is more generous than people."

Mr. Braverman was a communist. He argued that

property should be distributed justly. It was wrong for the rich to have everything, while the poor didn't have a crust of bread. He suffered because of his opinions. The police used to come to the school and arrest him from time to time, and he would spend a few months in prison. After he signed a statement saying he wouldn't spread his ideas anymore, they allowed him to teach music again. He would be careful not to express his opinions, but sometimes a hint would slip out—and they would immediately suspend him from the school.

"I like Mr. Braverman. I don't have a good ear, and my eyesight is poor. Mr. Braverman consoled me by saying, 'But you think well. Don't worry. Everyone has his own area.' A marvelous man," said Thomas, near tears.

Chapter 21

The rain didn't stop, and shooting sliced into the night and shook the nest. As soon as the rain let up, they went down to see whether the cow and calf were grazing in the meadow. They weren't. But Mina had left two slices of bread and some cheese. This time they were wrapped in cardboard.

They climbed back into the nest, had their meal, and were happy. Miro was also excited and hopped from Adam's feet to Thomas's.

"Thomas, would you please write a little letter to Mina?"

"What should I write?" Thomas asked. "I can't write 'Dear Mina.' No one may know that she has friends. I'll simply write: 'Thanks from A. and T.'"

"Maybe you should write, 'Blessings and thanks from A. and T.,'" said Adam.

"I've never used the word 'blessings,'" said Thomas.

"It's a beautiful word," said Adam.

"But not understandable. I'm not used to writing words that I don't understand. I propose writing, 'Thanks with all our hearts, from A. and T.'"

"Why are you so precise, Thomas?"

"What can I do? That's the way I was raised."

The nights were cold and not quiet. Sometimes it seemed to them that the teacher, Mr. Braverman, was still lying on the grass and groaning with pain. Every once in a while the steps of a man fleeing were heard as he looked for cover in the forest.

How can we help people? Adam asked himself. We have to help people.

Suddenly before his eyes he saw his mother, working in the communal kitchen in the ghetto, serving soup to thin, weak people. When they asked whether there was another crust of bread, she would narrow her shoulders and say, "I have none. Not a crumb is left." At night she would return from the communal kitchen exhausted and fall onto her bed. Thomas's parents believed in studying. They taught the Jewish children who had been suspended from school and made sure they did their homework. They said, "They can starve us, but they can't take our humanity away from us."

Thomas's father not only taught the Jewish children who had been suspended from school. He also organized courses in history, literature, and even a class in drawing for adults. From time to time he raised his voice and said, "Barbarity won't deter us." Not everyone agreed with him. Some people made fun of him and called him strange names, but that didn't stop him. Day and night he organized and taught, until he was seized for forced labor.

Chapter 22

Afterward the nights were quiet, and for a while it seemed there were no more fugitives. The bread and cheese nourished them and Miro. Between one rainstorm and another they would come down from the nest and sneak in to milk the cow.

Adam said, "God only knows how much Mina has been risking for our sake."

Thomas answered, "I've also been thinking about that."

"Are we worthy of her risk?" asked Adam.

"We'll do our best to be worthy," said Thomas with emotion.

"We underestimated her when she was with us in school," said Adam.

"The conclusion: You mustn't look down on people. Not on anyone," said Thomas.

"And you have to repeat the words of Brother

Peter, the religion teacher: 'Every man bears a message in his heart,'" said Adam.

Again at night they heard the stumbling steps of someone fleeing and the running of his pursuers. From the treetop they saw the struggle between the weak and the strong, and their hearts were full of dread.

Adam said, "We can't stand idly by. We have to help the fugitives."

Thomas didn't ignore Adam's words. When he saw a man fleeing, carrying a baby in his arms, he stuck his head out of the nest and called out loudly, "Don't be afraid, and don't lose hope. The Red Army is on its way to us. In a little while, a day or two."

The escaping man didn't stop to see who was encouraging him but kept on running, out of breath, but the armed pursuers raised their heads. They heard Thomas's shouts and shot at the nest.

"We have to get out of here," said Adam.

"Sorry," said Thomas. "I couldn't control myself."

"No matter. A word of encouragement is sometimes like a bandage."

"Thanks," said Thomas.

The thought flashed through Adam's mind: Thomas minds his manners, even when he is tense. In the last darkness, they folded their blan-

kets and the sheepskin coat, closed their backpacks, climbed down from the tree, and blazed
a trail into the thick forest. In an hour they saw
a tree with a round top. They immediately gathered twigs and branches, Adam climbed up, and
Thomas handed him what they had collected.
Now they were deep in the forest, far from the
paths, and Thomas wondered whether they had
gotten too far from the cow and calf and from the
tree where Mina placed the food.

Adam said, "I know the forest and everything
in it."

Chapter 23

While they were curling up in the new nest, the rain started again. First slowly, then heavily. The sheepskin coat, which had absorbed a lot of rain, was heavy and cold now. If it hadn't been for Miro, their situation would have been more serious. Miro not only gave off heat, but also happiness.

"I noticed that Miro is different from us but still similar to us," said Thomas.

"I just love Miro the way he is," said Adam.

Thomas was surprised once more by Adam's direct way of thinking. He didn't complain, didn't argue, but just acted. There was a lot to be learned from him.

Meanwhile the thunder in the distance got louder. It was hard to know whether it was the thunder of a storm or the booming of cannons. The rain didn't let up. A fugitive collapsed nearby, and his groaning rose to the treetop. Adam and Thomas took some iodine and bandages, climbed down from the tree, and approached the wounded man.

When he saw the boys, he raised his head and cried out, "Who are you? How did you get here?"

"My name is Adam, and my friend's name is Thomas. We've been hiding out in the forest."

"I'm wounded, dear children. Thank you for your willingness to help me."

"If we see the wound, we can bandage it. We have iodine, too," Adam said softly.

"Good angels. I can't believe my eyes."

"We also have a thermos bottle with clean water. We can wash the wound. Then we'll disinfect it with iodine."

Without hesitation they rolled up his sleeve and immediately saw the wound. Adam wiped off the blood and washed the wound. Thomas spread iodine on it. The stinging was severe, and the man bit his lips in pain.

They sat around him, together with Miro.

"Who are you?" the man asked again.

Adam stated their names.

"I know your parents, Adam. I own a furniture store, and I buy your father's handiwork. Your father is a wonderful craftsman."

"Did you see our mothers, perhaps?" Thomas asked.

"The commotion in the railroad station was huge. It was the last transport. My parents urged me to flee, and I left them to their fate. I'll never forgive myself."

"Was that long ago?"

"Quite a few days have already passed. Since then they've been running after me. Children, go back to your hiding place. I'll go look for somewhere to hide. You can already hear the booming of cannons in the distance. The Red Army is approaching. Hold on!"

Still they managed to persuade him to eat some corn pie and drink some water. Finally they left him and went away.

Thomas didn't stop dreaming. "In my dream I saw Dad coming back from the war. I said to him right away, 'Dad, forgive me for not reading the books I took with me, and I didn't solve the arithmetic problems.' Dad looked at me and said, 'Don't be sorry. Right after the war, studies will resume, and we'll do everything we can to make up for what you missed.' Strange, I said to myself. Dad is still concerned with my studies, even though he got thin and can barely stand up. 'I'm sorry,' I said again. 'It wasn't your fault, son.' He uttered those words and disappeared. A strange dream, right, Adam?"

"I also dream sometimes," said Adam. "But I forget my dreams."

"You're lucky. I dream almost every night. Mom says that the dreams are trying to guide us, to show us what to do. They are our conscience."

"I don't know what to say to you," said Adam. That was a sentence Adam repeated every time Thomas raised a complicated issue. By now Thomas knew Adam's ways, but he kept asking questions and raising difficulties.

Thomas's questions sometimes amused Adam. Once Adam said to him, "Next time choose a friend who can answer all your questions."

As they were making their way to the cow and calf, an old peasant appeared as though he had sprung from the earth, and he alarmed them. The peasant also seemed surprised, and he asked, "Who are you?"

Adam took heart and answered him. "My name is Adam, and my friend's name is Thomas."

"Are you Jewish children?" asked the peasant.

"Yes," said Adam, taking two steps backward.

"And you're not afraid?"

"A little," Adam admitted.

"In a little while the Red Army will come, and you can go home. You can already hear the cannons."

"When will that be?" Adam asked.

"Very soon," said the peasant, taking a piece of brown cake from his coat pocket and offering it to Adam.

"Thanks, grandfather."

"You don't have to thank me, but God. Children, hide well. The Germans are in every corner. Don't leave your hiding place. I'll leave a bit of food at the foot of this tree now and then. When the day of victory arrives, come and visit me."

"What's your name, Grandfather?"

"My name is Sergei."

They cleared out and climbed the tree. Miro couldn't repress his joy. He hopped from foot to foot, hoping to get a piece of cake. It was a delicious honey cake, and they finished it immediately. The water they sipped from the thermos bottle was tastier than ever.

Chapter 24

From then on the rain didn't stop. It was accompanied by thunder and lightning, as well as hail, which struck the cloak very hard. Without Miro and his body heat, they would have been frozen.

"Who's that old man we met, Sergei?" Adam asked. "Do you mean to say he was sent to us?" asked Thomas.

"I don't know whether he was sent to us. I'm glad he appeared."

"My dad says, 'A person should do what he must do.' If only I knew exactly what I'm supposed to do," said Thomas.

"We do what we can," said Adam.

"I'm not reading the books I brought with me, and I'm not solving arithmetic problems. I hardly even write in my journal."

"Don't worry, Thomas. When the war is over, you'll catch up on everything."

"It's a shame to waste time," said Thomas.

"But you saw a lot. You were hungry a lot. You were afraid and you overcame your fear. That's also learning, isn't it?"

The rain fell without stopping, and they didn't climb down from the tree. They lay down tensely. Adam talked to Miro and asked him how he was feeling. Miro murmured and whined in little yips. From time to time he would jump down from the tree and look around in the forest.

Miro was a brave guard. Once, back home, he gripped a thief's arm and wouldn't let go. The thief was desperate and shouted, "Help!" If it hadn't been for Adam's father, who released the thief's arm from Miro's teeth, he might not have survived. After he was released, the thief didn't move, as though he were hypnotized. "Go away and don't come back," Adam's father scolded him, and then he did pick up his feet and run away.

During a letup, they climbed down to see whether Mina had left them anything. To their surprise they found a packet wrapped in canvas near the tree where they had met the peasant.

They quickly carried it up to the nest, and to their astonishment they found a big piece of corn pie, a hunk of cheese, and a packet of pickled cucumbers.

"Is everything that happens to us coincidental?" Adam wondered.

"Do you have a better word than that?" Thomas answered.

"We met marvelous people who saved us. Is that all a coincidence?"

"Why say they were sent to us? Why not say they're doing it of their own free will?"

"I don't know what to say to you," said Adam.

They had a meal and shared it with Miro. Everything was delicious, especially the pickles. The canvas wasn't big, but it covered them.

"We haven't seen Mina for a while," said Thomas.

"Peasants don't go out to the fields or pastures in the rain. But sometimes it seems to me that they're hurting her. I hope I'm wrong," said Adam.

"Where did you get that impression?"

"It's hard to explain," said Adam.

That day Thomas wrote in his journal:

Dear Mother and Father,

Adam and I are still hiding out in the forest. The rain doesn't stop, but don't worry. We're curled up in our nest. We have a sheepskin cloak, the blankets we brought from home, and a piece of canvas to shield us. I think about you all the time, I see you in dreams, and when I'm awake, and I hope you're well. I have a feeling that the war is ending, and we'll come home. My friend Adam is a perfect friend. We live from day to day and wonders keep astonishing us. An old peasant we met by chance left us a whole corn pie. Adam says we must say blessings. Adam's a nature boy, but at the same time he has a sense of the marvelous. I've learned a lot from him. Now I also know how to run in a crouch and climb trees. Sometimes it seems to me that my outward appearance has changed a lot since we parted. I hope that I've stayed the same Thomas you used to know. You're in my thoughts every day. I'm waiting with yearning for the end of the war and for the moment I can come down from the tree, straight to you.

Adam remembered the apple tree, and they ran to it. The apples had turned red, and some of them had fallen to the earth. They picked apples and gathered them in the canvas. Miro didn't leave their side. From time to time he raised his head, turned it, and pointed his nose.

Between rainstorms they went down to Mina's tree. This time they found a few pieces of bread and a piece of butter wrapped in a rag.

The last time they saw Mina, her right hand had been bandaged in a kerchief. She milked the cow quickly, so it didn't seem like a serious injury to them. But Adam kept repeating, "The peasant is not only angry at her. He beats her."

"How do you know?"

"From the expression on her lips. The next time we meet her we should ask her to join us," said Adam.

"Let's hope she won't be afraid to run away," said Thomas.

"Mina's a brave girl. Look at her hands as she milks."

The next day they found Mina milking. Adam directed his voice at her and called out, "If things are hard for you, and if the peasant is hurting you, come to us. We have a nest in a tall tree, and, if necessary, we can flee into the heart of the forest. We don't have a lot to eat, but whatever comes our way is enough to live on. If you want to join us, we'd be very happy."

Mina heard, but her face didn't move. When she finished milking, she took the pail and the stool and hurried away.

When Mina went away, she left behind a trail of secrecy. She was so short and so small, it was a wonder she could carry the heavy pail. "She's a spirit, not a body," said Adam.

"Where did you get that feeling, Adam?" asked Thomas.

"The pail is as big as half her body. Who's carrying the pail, if not the spirit that's in her?"

"For years in school we never realized she was a being with spiritual strength."

"Our eyes deceive us," said Adam, and they both laughed.

Chapter 25

After that dark days came. Cold filled the forest, and rain mixed with hail pounded the canvas.

Every time thunder and lightning exploded above them, Miro pricked up his ears.

"Is the war drawing to a close?" Adam asked Miro and looked at his face.

Miro couldn't stay still. Every few minutes he stuck his head out of the canvas and let out little barks.

Snow was not long in coming. First it was mixed with rain, but from day to day it thickened and grew whiter. Mina continued to leave packages next to her tree. Once it was a packet of dry fruit. The good peasant left them a jug of buttermilk.

"What would we have done without our angels?" said Adam.

It snowed harder, and the cold grew fiercer.

Adam and Thomas wore the shirts, the sweaters, and the coats that they had, but the cold wind penetrated their clothing.

Adam kept asking Miro if he sensed that the Red Army was advancing. Miro raised his head, pricked up his ears, and muttered dissatisfied little barks. He was complaining about the weather, which made it hard for him to sense things.

Their new enemy was now the cold and the wind. They had to reinforce the nest, add branches, and carefully build thick walls around the nest with twigs. One day from above they saw Mina come out of the darkness of the forest, place a package on the snow, and go away. Her movements were light, gliding, and hardly touched the snow. Fresh snow filled her footprints right away.

"Think of how much courage she needs to wrap corn pie and cheese in paper and sneak out of the house," said Thomas.

"She's a girl from out of this world," said Adam, and he was alarmed by the words he had said.

They climbed down to see what Mina had left them. This time the package held a piece of cake, a slice of bread, and two sugar cubes.

"I have the feeling that Mina baked this cake."

"How come?" asked Thomas.

"My heart tells me."

"The cold is getting worse. Maybe we should go to Diana's," said Thomas.

Adam looked at Thomas and said, "It's not right to leave the forest in this difficult time. The forest has protected us all the time, and I have a feeling that we can hold out without Diana."

"The cold is penetrating to my fingers and biting them."

"The cold is getting to me, too. We have to rub our fingers," said Adam, and he added, "We've been in the forest for many months. We overcame fear and want. Now we have two angels who watch over us, and for our part we'll do everything to overcome the cold."

"Adam, you constantly amaze me."

The snow didn't stop falling. Thick flakes streamed thickly down from the sky. From time to time thunderbolts ripped the heavens. Miro was tense. Adam stopped him from jumping out, getting into danger. He spoke to him softly, saying, "Miro, it's horrible outside. It's best for you to be up here in the nest, to curl up under the blankets. When we're together, the warmth stays, do you understand?"

Thomas wrote in his notebook:

Dear Mom and Dad,

The snow doesn't stop falling. It's piled high. If I'm not mistaken, half a meter. But don't worry. We've improved our nest. We put on all the clothes we have. I think about you all the time, but since I don't know where you are or what you're doing, my thoughts wander somewhere else every time. Fortune favored us, and our friend Mina and the peasant we met by chance bring food to us. My friend Adam calls them angels. The booming in the distance can be heard very well. Let's hope it brings the Red Army on its wings. Conditions are hard, but we haven't lost hope. Last night I dreamed you were liberated and had come to pick up me and Adam. You were very thin, but your faces expressed satisfaction. I hope so much it will be that way. Don't delay. Come. I love you very much, Thomas.

Thomas read what he had written to Adam. Adam listened and said, "You described the situation correctly. I don't know how to write the way you do."

"But you're better at making your way in nature than I am."

"Sometimes I have the feeling that my parents receive my thoughts," said Adam.

"It also seems that way to me, but I'm not sure," said Thomas.

"You have to be strong and trust yourself, Thomas. When we met you didn't know how to climb trees, you didn't know how to walk right in the forest, and now you're as agile and quick as a squirrel."

"I still haven't gotten to your level," said Thomas.

"There's no need to compete. Everyone has to be faithful to himself."

One cold night Thomas suddenly asked Adam, "What do you want to study, Adam?"

"I want to learn from my father."

"You want to be an expert carpenter?"

"Yes. And what do you want to study?" Adam asked.

"I'll go on to high school and college."

"Let's pray that the winds and snow will leave us alone, and that our parents will come and get us soon."

Upon hearing Adam's words, Thomas burst into tears.

Chapter 26

Miro startled them. He leaped out of the nest and raced toward the interior of the forest. Tensely they watched him run. Every few steps he would stand still, stretch out his head, listen, and sniff.

"Miro has sensed something. He wouldn't leap away for nothing," said Adam.

After an hour of scouting, he came back and stood next to the tree. Adam climbed down and carried him back up, rubbed his legs, and pressed him to his chest. Gradually warmth returned to Miro's body. "What happened, Miro? The cold outside is biting. Don't run any risks," Adam said to him. "Miro is different from us," he said to Thomas. "Sounds and smells come to him before they reach us."

"Did you learn anything from Miro's behavior in the past few days?" asked Thomas.

"It seems to me he's annoyed with himself because he can't catch the signs that come to him from far away."

"What should we do?" Thomas asked softly.

"If the snow keeps falling, and the cold gets stronger, we won't have any choice except to climb down and light a fire to keep warm."

"Won't the fire give us away?"

"We'll do it cautiously."

That night Adam heard his mother's trembling voice speaking to him. "My Adam, we have arrived. Don't be afraid. You know our forest very well, and everything that's in it. I'll try very hard to come in the evening."

Her voice was clear, as if she hadn't spoken months ago, but just now. Adam wakened from his slumber. Heavy snowflakes fell from the sky and filled the dark with gray whiteness. Thomas was sleeping deeply. Adam was afraid the cold would trap him in its web, and he woke him. Thomas asked, "What's the matter?"

"Nothing. Aren't you cold?"

"No."

"Try to move your toes."

"It's hard."

"Let's rub them so they won't freeze. Your toes can freeze easily when you're asleep."

Chapter 27

From above, in the last watch of the night, they saw a short creature, wrapped in a blanket, tottering and wandering in the snow. The tiny creature advanced with difficulty, stumbling with every few steps. Clearly it was about to faint, or it was wounded and trying to resist the wind that kept knocking it over.

They didn't delay but climbed down. They immediately saw that it was Mina.

Her face was bleeding. She was breathing with difficulty. Adam and Thomas held her and carried her to the tree, and carefully, from branch to branch, they carried her up to the nest and immediately started taking care of her.

"What happened to you, Mina? Don't be afraid. Thomas and I will watch over you."

Now that they had wrapped her up, once again they realized how light she was, almost weightless.

Meanwhile the thunder in the distance had stopped. It snowed harder from hour to hour. By now it was a meter deep. They curled up together. The blanket that Mina had brought with her helped to cover them. But the cold penetrated anyway, and it stung and hurt them.

"We won't have any choice but to go down and light a fire," said Adam.

"Maybe we should wait another day," said Thomas.

"We'll wait as long as we can, but no longer."

Meanwhile they rubbed their hands together, and they rubbed Mina's feet to draw her out of the cold and her weakness.

The peasant angel left them a pitcher of milk and half a loaf of bread. They put drops of milk in Mina's mouth. She opened her eyes for a moment and then quickly closed them.

Miro wouldn't stand still. The narrow space they were trying to seal off from the cold seemed to oppress him. A couple of times he was about to leap, but Adam stopped him.

Finally he freed himself and jumped. Adam wanted to run after him, but he realized he couldn't catch up with him. Miro raced quickly, as though pursued, into the interior of the forest. They watched him fearfully. The darkness, which had fallen, separated them from Miro.

"Where did Miro run to?" Thomas asked in a trembling voice.

"Miro wouldn't run off for no reason. Danger doesn't deter him."

Adam bent very close to Mina's face and whispered, "Just another small effort, Mina. We're getting close to the end of the war. In a little while, just a bit, the Red Army will come and liberate us."

Chapter 28

But the night continued, long and dark. The cold grew more intense from hour to hour. Mina wasn't breathing well. From time to time grunts of pain escaped her lips. Her mouth wouldn't accept liquids, and the boys were afraid for her life.

Adam said, "In the morning we'll go down and light a fire."

Thomas agreed with him. "We mustn't stay up in the nest and freeze."

Trembling with fear and shivering with cold, at the first light they saw two people in the distance, stumbling through the snow, and Miro was running in front of them.

"Miro," Adam called with all his strength.

Miro heard his voice and stood on his two hind legs, which was what he used to do when he had something to announce. "Miro," Adam called again in a voice that shook the nest.

They were about to climb down, but they didn't want to leave Mina alone. From above they observed the figures as they approached.

Fortunately the snow stopped and the visibility improved. Adam called out, "Mom!" and shook the nest.

"Are you sure?"

"I can see her."

They wrapped Mina in blankets and the canvas and slowly, from branch to branch, they brought her down.

They were about to run together to their mothers, but they stopped their legs.

When their mothers were close to them, with Miro in front of them, Thomas couldn't restrain himself and started running. He didn't get very far. The deep snow stopped him. Their mothers were also struggling with the snow. They advanced slowly. The distance between them and Thomas grew shorter, but still a gap remained.

Adam called out from where he was, "Mom, not much more, just a little bit."

The mothers arrived, out of breath, and fell onto the snow. Adam's mother let out a loud moan such as Adam had never heard from her. He gripped her and called out, "Mom, it's all over."

She managed to say, "My hero," before she fainted.

Adam put a few drops of milk on her lips. His mother opened her eyes and said, "Whom should I thank?"

Thomas's mother didn't say a word. Thomas hugged her hard and finally shook her and said, "Mom, why aren't you talking?"

Adam's mother asked, "Who's the girl on the twigs?"

Adam answered with a stifled voice, "She's Mina, a girl from out of this world. In the days when we had no food, she brought us bread and corn pie. She's sick, very sick. The peasant who hid her beat her and threw her out of the house."

"Good God!" said his mother. "We have to bring her to the Red Army infirmary right away. Where is the girl from?"

"She was in our class. We have to save her," Thomas said.

Adam told her, "She's our age, but she was always short. The peasant who hid her mistreated her, but she risked her life and brought us bread and corn pie, and thanks to her, Mom, we're alive."

"She's an angel. I have no doubt she's an angel," said his mother, and her head sank down.

Chapter 29

They didn't delay. They wrapped Mina in blankets, laid her on the canvas, and carried her. It was hard to advance. They had to stop every few steps.

"Thomas, forgive me for not coming to get you. I couldn't leave your grandparents to their fate. At the railroad station there was a commotion, and it was mobbed. Your grandparents could barely stand up."

"Mom, I forgive you with all my soul."

"I left you alone," her voice quivered.

"Fate sent Adam to me. He is my friend in heart and soul, and in the past months Mina brought us food." Thomas wanted to ask about his father and grandparents, but he stopped himself. Like Adam, he felt they had to save Mina first.

After walking for two hours, trying to put a

few drops of milk in Mina's mouth, they reached the infirmary of the Red Army.

"Who are you?" asked the doctor, a tall, thin man. He wore glasses and looked like Brother Peter in their school.

Thomas's mother answered: "We're Jews, and we're mothers. We were in camps, and our children hid in the forest. Our daughter is sick and she was beaten. The peasant who hid her abused her, hit her, and finally threw her out into the cold."

"We'll examine her immediately," said the doctor.

Now they could see the blue bruises and red welts on her little body.

The doctor was shocked by the seriousness of her wounds and called out, "Good God, there's no limit to cruelty," and he instructed a nurse to wash her.

"Sit down. We'll do everything we can to save this precious little girl." He asked one of the medics to give them soup and a piece of bread.

For a long time not a sound was heard in the infirmary. The mothers wanted to know everything that had happened to Adam and Thomas during their long months in the forest, but fatigue and weakness overcame them, and they fell asleep.

At noon the doctor emerged from the infirmary and said, "The girl opened her eyes, and that's a good sign. We'll keep an eye on her for the time being. How old is the child?"

"She's nine," Thomas's mother answered.

"Good God! Only a man without God in his soul is capable of such cruelty," said the doctor.

"Will Mina recover from her illness?" Thomas's mother asked in a trembling voice.

"With God's help," the doctor answered. He looked more and more like the school priest.

The cold outside was fierce, but it was warm in the tent. The doctor stood and looked at them with wonder. Adam felt like saying, "Again we met an angel, this time in the figure of a doctor," but he didn't say it.

The next day the doctor didn't deny that there were some hard moments in bringing Mina back to life. In the end the good angels won out. The girl was out of danger.

"Thank God," said Thomas's mother.

"Thank the medical team that made an effort," the doctor replied.

Adam's mother was alarmed by the doctor's correction and said, "Sorry."

That night the doctor announced, "The girl, thank God, is showing good signs of recovery."

"Is she talking?" Adam's mother asked. "She's talking a little."

"Can you understand what she's saying?"

"Absolutely."

"Thank God," said Adam's mother in the doctor's tone of voice.

All that day Adam and Thomas told about their life in the forest, about the raspberries and blueberries, about the brook, about the nest that protected them day and night, about Mina who had saved them from hunger, and about the old peasant who brought them bread and milk during the final hard days.

"I didn't read, and I didn't solve arithmetic exercises, but I kept a diary," Thomas told his mother. "But it's all broken up. We'll only be able to tell about what happened to us in the forest for a few years."

Thomas's mother opened her eyes wide. Thomas's words frightened her, and she said, "What do you mean by saying you won't be able to tell about what happened to you in the forest for a few years?"

Thomas answered, "It's hard to talk about fear and hunger. They are very concrete, but indescribable."

When she heard his words, her eyes filled with tears.

Meanwhile the doctor came out and said, "Come in and see our pretty little girl. She's not only pretty, she's also a heroine."

Mina was lying in bed, her head raised on two pillows. Her eyes were open. Her beauty glowed from within her.

"How are you, Mina?" Adam's mother asked, trembling all over.

After a short silence she answered, "Well."

Adam's mother didn't ask any more questions.

"The medical team has fallen in love with Mina," said the doctor, and his face filled with light.

Chapter 30

They stayed in the infirmary tent for five days, constantly waiting in fear for the doctor's announcements. The medic didn't neglect them. He brought them soup, bread, and hard-boiled eggs. On the fifth day the doctor told them, "The girl is talking, asking questions and responding. She's a girl from out of this world. You'll have to keep bandaging her wounds. I'll give you anti-septic and salve. The wounds are healing, but you mustn't neglect treatment. The medical staff is impressed by Mina and wishes her a full recovery. You should know that she's a miracle in every way. And you, where are you going?"

"We don't know yet," answered one of the mothers.

"We'll give you some food to last for a few days."

"Thank you, doctor. I can't thank you enough."

"We're doing our duty as human beings. Tomorrow we're moving from here. We've broken through the front. The German army is retreating in panic, but the way to victory is still long. I'll give you a stretcher so you can carry Mina. She conquered all of our hearts."

"How can we thank you, doctor?" Adam's mother said, trying to restrain her tears.

"There's no need to thank us. We're here to do our duty."

"You treated us with mercy. It's been a long time since we saw mercy."

"I'm just a doctor. You mustn't attribute qualities to people that we attribute to God."

"I'm sorry if I insulted you. I didn't mean to," she said, covering her face with both hands.

Thus they parted from the doctor who had saved them.

The sun came out from behind the clouds and lit up the snow. The snow absorbed the sun from above and glowed with thousands of points of light.

A military band played marches in the middle of the snowy forest. Thomas's mother burst into tears, and Adam's mother hugged her, saying, "Dear, thank God we found the boys. Now we have to take care of Mina. She needs a lot of attention."

"Excuse me," Thomas's mother murmured and wiped her face.

The band continued to inspire joy.

Adam's mother said, "Who watched over our children in this hard winter?"

"Our boys are smart. They took care of themselves," said Thomas's mother.

Adam wanted to ask how his father was, and how his grandparents were, but he blocked the words in his mouth. In his heart he knew it wasn't the right time to ask. His mother sensed what was stirring in her son's heart and said, "Let's pray that Dad and your grandparents will return to us."

Mina fell asleep on the stretcher, and the mothers wrapped her in the blanket.

About the Author

First championed in the English language by Irving Howe and Philip Roth, AHARON APPELFELD was born in a village near Czernowitz, Bukovina, in 1932. During World War II, he was deported to a concentration camp in Transnistria, but escaped. He was eight years old. For the next three years, he wandered the forests. In 1944, he was picked up by the Red Army, served in field kitchens in Ukraine, then made his way to Italy. He reached Palestine in 1946. Today, Appelfield is professor emeritus of Hebrew literature at Ben-Gurion University at Beersheva, a member of the American Academy of Arts & Sciences, and commandeur de l'Ordre des Arts et des Lettres. He has won numerous prizes, including the Israel Prize, the MLA Commonwealth Award in Literature, the Prix Médicis étranger in France, the Premio Grinzane Cavour and Premio Boccaccio Internazionale, the Bertha von Suttner Award for Culture and Peace, and the 2012 Independent Foreign Fiction Prize. In 2013, he was a finalist for the Man Booker International Prize.

About the Translator

JEFFREY M. GREEN began to translate for Aharon Appelfeld in the 1980s and has translated a dozen or so of his novels. Green is the author of *Thinking Through Translation* (University of Georgia Press), as well as short stories, poems, novels, book reviews, and essays.

About the Illustrator

PHILIPPE DUMAS is an an author and illustrator of dozens of books for children and adults. A graduate of the École des Beaux Arts in Paris, he divides his time between illustration and set design for the theater.

About Seven Stories Press

SEVEN STORIES PRESS is an independent book publisher based in New York City. We publish works of the imagination by such writers as Nelson Algren, Russell Banks, Octavia E. Butler, Ani DiFranco, Assia Djebar, Ariel Dorfman, Coco Fusco, Barry Gifford, Martha Long, Luis Negrón, Hwang Sok-yong, Lee Stringer, and Kurt Vonnegut, to name a few, together with political titles by voices of conscience, including Subhankar Banerjee, the Boston Women's Health Collective, Noam Chomsky, Angela Y. Davis, Human Rights Watch, Derrick Jensen, Ralph Nader, Loretta Napoleoni, Gary Null, Greg Palast, Project Censored, Barbara Seaman, Alice Walker, Gary Webb, and Howard Zinn, among many others. Seven Stories Press believes publishers have a special responsibility to defend free speech and human rights, and to celebrate the gifts of the human imagination, wherever we can. In 2012 we launched Triangle Square books for young readers with strong social justice and narrative components, telling personal stories of courage and commitment. For additional information, visit www.sevenstories.com.